8

THIS BOOK BELONGS TO:

Other Kipper books

Kipper
Kipper's Toybox
Kipper's Birthday
Kipper's Snowy Day
Where, Oh Where, is Kipper's Bear?
Kipper's Book of Colours
Kipper's Book of Opposites
Kipper's Book of Counting
Kipper's Book of Weather

Butterfly

Mick Inkpen

h

Hodder
Children's
Books

A division of Hodder Headline plc

Kipper was trying to
catch a butterfly.
A little blue one.
   It landed on Pig's lolly.
And flew away again.
   'You'll never catch it,'
said Pig.

The butterfly flew to
the top of a lilac bush.
Kipper climbed up.
He made a grab. . .

. . .and missed!

In the park
in a pushchair
was a baby
with a balloon
which is where
the butterfly
came to rest
next.

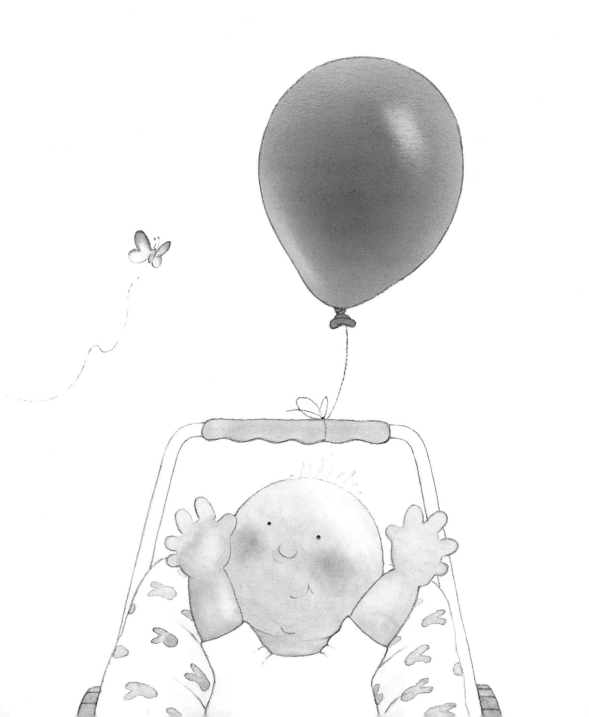

Kipper crept up
very quietly.
Closer and closer.
And closer still.
Very close indeed.

That was when
the balloon burst!

K ipper looked at the
balloon. He went
back to the lilac bush and
looked at the blossom.
   Then he went back to
Pig and said,
   'Show me your tongue!'

They were all . . .

...PURPLE!

K ipper made a
    pointed, purple,
paper hat.

He put it on Pig.

'What's this for?'
said Pig.

'Shhh!' said Kipper.

They didn't have
long to wait.

The little blue
butterfly landed
on Pig's hat.
Kipper closed
his paws
around it.
He had
caught it
at last!

Later though...

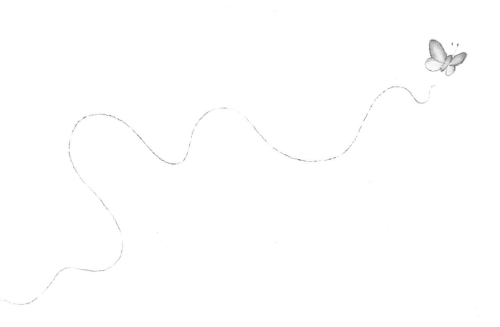

. . . he let it go.

First published 1999
by Hodder Children's Books,
a division of Hodder Headline plc,
338 Euston Road, London NW1 3BH

Copyright © Mick Inkpen 1999

10 9 8 7 6 5 4 3 2 1

ISBN 0 340 736925

Printed in Hong Kong